WE CAN READ!™

Luau

by Jacqueline Sweeney

photography by G. K. & Vikki Hart
photo illustration by Blind Mice Studio

BENCHMARK BOOKS

MARSHALL CAVENDISH
NEW YORK

For Jerry Thomas, who understands how all 'dancers' are becoming the dance and that most of us are 'Eddie'!

With thanks to Daria Murphy, principal of Scotchtown Elementary School, Goshen, New York, and former reading specialist, for reading this manuscript with care and for writing the "We Can Read and Learn" activity guide.

Benchmark Books
Marshall Cavendish
99 White Plains Road
Tarrytown, New York 10591
www.marshallcavendish.com

Text copyright © 2003 by Jacqueline Sweeney
Photo illustrations © 2003 by G.K. & Vikki Hart
and Mark and Kendra Empey

Library of Congress Cataloging-in-Publication Data
Sweeney, Jacqueline.
Luau / by Jacqueline Sweeney ; photography by G.K. and Vikki Hart ; photo illustrations by Blind Mice Studio.
p. cm. -- (We can read!)
Summary: The animal friends at Willow Pond make a luau after they receive a letter showing them how from a friend in Hawaii.
ISBN 0-7614-1513-0
[1. Luaus--Fiction. 2. Parties--Fiction. 3. Animals--Fiction.] I. Hart, G. K., ill. II. Hart, Vikki, ill. III. Title.
PZ7.S974255 Lu 2002   [E]--dc21   2002003239

Printed in Italy

1 3 5 6 4 2

Characters

Tim

Eddie

Jim

Ron

The Bunnies

The Owls

A yellow box sat on Pond Rock.

Tim jumped inside.

"Presents!" he yelled.

"Molly sent them
from Hawaii."

Tim held up puka shells.

Eddie pulled out a grass skirt.

Jim found a letter.

He read it out loud.

Dear Makamaka,

I'm sending all you need

for a Willow Pond luau.

Have fun!

Love,

Molly

P.S. Send pictures!

"What's a makamaka?" asked Tim.

"And a luau?" asked Jim.

"Makamaka means friends," said Ron.

"A luau is a feast."

"Count me in!" said Eddie.

"I love to eat.

But how do we make it?"

"That's easy," said Ron.

"Molly gave us jobs."

He handed each friend a list.

Tim,

Get your family to
help you dig a big hole.
You need a hole 3 feet
3 feet to cook in.

Molly

"I'm in charge of guests,"
croaked Ron.
"I'll ask the owls to help."
He leaped down Pebble Path.

Tim,
Get your family to
help you dig a big hole.
You need a hole 3 feet
by 3 feet to cook in.
Molly

"I'm in charge of digging,"
said Tim.

"We'll need a pit for the fire.
I'll need more feet."

He hopped towards Bunny Hollow.

J.P.,

You're in charge of
kau-kau. Gather the
food and fruit from the
box and prepare it.

Jolly

"And I'm in charge of kau-kau,"
said Jim.
"I think that means food."

"I have the best job of all,"
said Eddie.
He just smiled and
walked slowly off.

The next day was busy.

The bunnies were digging.

Ron was writing notes.

The owls were making leis.

Jim was filling bowls.

At last the fire was lit.
The food was cooking.
The log table was set.

"Where's Eddie?" asked Tim.
But no one knew.

Suddenly a shape leaped
from the darkness
onto Pond Rock.

The friends heard
a blast of sound.

It was Eddie!

He was blowing into a large shell.

"Let the luau begin!" he cried.

"I'm in charge of the hula."

And he started to dance.

First he moved his body.
Then he moved his arms.

The crickets sang:

Mahalo, ahi lani kai.

Thank you, fire and sea and sky.

Mahalo, rain and flowers and sun.

Mahalo, Molly for this fun.

Eddie whirled and leaped
and swayed.
He moved his hands
to show the rain.
He moved his arms
to show the sky.
"Makamaka,
now you try!"

All the friends began to dance.

And they sang:

Aloha wai pua la.

Hello to rain and flowers and sun.

Thank you, lovely sea and sky.

Mahalo, nani lani kai.

WE CAN READ AND LEARN

The following activities, which complement *Luau*, are designed to help children build skills in vocabulary, phonics, critical thinking, and creative writing.

CHALLENGE WORDS

The Hawaiian alphabet has only twelve letters—five vowels (a, e, i, o, u) and seven consonants (h, k, l, m, n, p, w). The vowels are pronounced as follows: **a**—*ah* as in father; **e**—*eh* as in bet; **i**—*ee* as in see; **o**—*oh* as in sole; **u**--*oo* as in moon. Help children pronounce the Hawaiian words that appear in *Luau*. Then discuss their meanings.

makamaka	kau-kau	hula	aloha
lani	luau	leis	mahalo
ahi	kai	wai	pua
nani	la		

Help children figure out the meanings of the following English words by focusing on the contexts in *Luau* in which they appear.

presents	towards	strange	deep
charge	blast	pit	whirled
suddenly	shape	darkness	leaped

FUN WITH PHONICS

Cut out fifteen different shell shapes from construction paper. Next, cut out three extra-large shell shapes. On the first extra-large shell write: OU (round). On the second extra-large shell write: OW (snow). On the third extra-large shell write: OW (cow). Write the following words from *Luau* on the fifteen small shells (one word per shell): found, out, loud, count, sound, hollow, yellow, willow, bowl, blow, how, now, owls, flowers, down.

Tape the three large shells to a wall. Read aloud the words and letters printed on each shell, explaining that the three shells represent different word families. Make a pile of the fifteen smaller shells and shuffle them. Lift a small shell so that you can see the word printed on it but the children cannot. Read aloud the word printed on it. Have the children guess the shell family to which the small shell belongs. Turn the small shell around to reveal the spelling of the word you have just read. Then tape the small shell under the large shell representing the family to which it belongs. Repeat until all of the small shells have been taped under the large shells.

LUAU AT WILLOW POND

A luau is a Hawaiian tradition. It is a feast to celebrate great accomplishments, to honor an important person, or to commemorate a special event. Help children prepare their very own luau. Like the friends at Willow Pond, each child could have a specific job. The ideas below will help make your luau as much fun as the one in the story.

• Use tiny sea shells (or pasta shells) to create necklaces for each child. Plastic lacing (lanyard) is easy to use for stringing the shells.

• Grass skirts can be made from sheets of green paper or crepe paper streamers. Cut the paper into long strips and glue the ends onto a strip of felt or sturdy paper. Tie this strip around a child's waist.

• No luau is complete without Hawaiian food. Some of the recipes from these cookbooks are simple enough for young children to follow with your help:

Keao, Mae. *Cooking with Hawaiian Magic: At Last!: Island Recipes and Luau Ideas for Our Mainland Friends.* Honolulu, Hawaii: Island Book Shelf, 1990.

Monroe, Elvira. *Hawaii, Cooking with Aloha.* San Carlos, CA: Wide World Publishing/Tetra, 1993.

Schindler, Roana and Gene. *Hawaiian Cookbook.* New York: Dover Publications, 1985.

• To make leis, cut bright-colored tissue paper into small squares. Bunch up each square. Help children use a needle to thread the bunched-up tissue paper onto a string. Each lei will require twenty to thirty bunched-up tissue squares.

HULA GAME

Hula was once part of Hawaiian religious ceremonies and is now generally a form of entertainment. Each movement in a hula has a specific meaning. Usually the movements represent things in nature such as palm trees, sharks, birds, and waves.

Have children agree upon four or five objects or phenomena found in nature that would be easy to represent in a dance. Once dance movements corresponding to the things in nature have been decided upon, you can play the hula game. Call out the names of the objects or phenomena. When you do the children should respond with the corresponding movements. You should aim to eventually call the names in very quick succession, so that following along becomes a real challenge.

About the author

Jacqueline Sweeney is a poet and children's author. She has worked with children and teachers for over twenty-five years implementing writing workshops in schools throughout the United States. She specializes in motivating reluctant writers and shares her creative teaching methods in numerous professional books for teachers. Her most recent work includes the Benchmark Books series *Kids Express*, a series of anthologies of poetry and art by children, which she conceived of and edited. She lives in Catskill, New York.

About the photo illustrations

The photo illustrations are the collaborative effort of photographers G. K. and Vikki Hart and Mark and Kendra Empey of Blind Mice Studio. Following Mark Empey's sketched storyboard, G. K. and Vikki Hart photograph each animal and element individually. The images are then scanned and manipulated, pixel by pixel, by Mark and Kendra Empey at Blind Mice Studio. Each charming illustration may contain from 15 to 30 individual photographs.

All the animals that appear in this book were handled with love. They have been returned to or adopted by loving homes.